ONE
MEAN
ANT
WITH
FLY
AND
FLEA

For Les and Sandy,
my most cherished friends

AY

To Herman and Maura

SR

Text copyright © 2020 by Arthur Yorinks
Illustrations copyright © 2020 by Sergio Ruzzier

First edition 2020

Library of Congress Catalog Card Number pending
ISBN 978-0-7636-8395-5

20 21 22 23 24 25 CCP 10 9 8 7 6 5 4 3 2 1

Printed in Shenzhen, Guangdong, China

This book was typeset in ITC American Typewriter.
The illustrations were done in pen and ink and watercolor.

Candlewick Press
99 Dover Street
Somerville, Massachusetts 02144

www.candlewick.com

ONE MEAN ANT

— WITH —

FLY AND FLEA

written by
Arthur Yorinks

illustrated by
Sergio Ruzzier

CANDLEWICK PRESS

Ah, there they were . . . one mean ant and his friend, the fly, both stuck in a spider's web, both on the menu for the spider's upcoming dinner.

"Ant . . ." the fly whimpered.

"What now? Haven't you done enough?" asked the ant.

"I don't want to be food!" cried the fly. "I'm too young to be eaten!"

"Well, you should have thought of that when you got us into this mess," said the ant. "You flew us right into this web!"

You see, the fly was flying, carrying the ant out of the desert and—well, that's another story.

"Ant," said the fly.

"Oh, do you have to keep talking?" the ant asked.

"I guess not. I don't have to keep talking, but—" replied the fly.

"But *what*?" growled the mean ant.

"But I see a spot," continued the fly.

"Good for you!" The ant was not a happy ant.

"It's moving!" said the fly. "The spot is coming closer."

"Oh no! It's the s-spider!" said the ant. "It's coming for us. It's going to eat us!"

"Well, it's a pretty small spider," said the fly. "Maybe—"

"Are you blind?" asked the ant. "That spider is—uh, that spider will—I mean it's . . . oh. It's not a spider. It's just a spot." The ant was relieved.

"Hey! Spot!" he called out. "Who are you?"

"Don't you mean *what* are you?" the fly whispered.

"Will you be quiet? I'm trying to find out what that spot is and . . . oh, all right." The ant sighed. "Spot!" he yelled. "*What* are you?"

"Who, me?" asked the spot, who was not a spot, but a flea.

"Yes, you!" shouted the ant. "Of course, you! You flea-brain!"

"Exactly!" said the flea.

"You see," said the fly, "it's an exactly. Whatever that is."

"No, no, I'm not a spot *or* an exactly. I'm a flea," said the flea.

"You're an appetizer now," said the ant. "The spider will eat you first, and then us."

"Oooh, oooh!" the fly said excitedly. "Maybe after eating the flea, the spider won't be hungry anymore."

"Are you nuts?" asked the ant. "Eating the flea first will only make the spider hungrier. We're cooked!"

"I don't think so. I don't see any pots or pans," said the fly.

"It's an expression! Do me a favor, just don't talk, I beg you. I'd rather face the music—"

"I don't hear any music," said the fly.

"Holy cannoli!" said the ant. "We're doomed, stuck like bugs in a rug."

"We're stuck in a web," the fly began. "We're not stuck in a—"

"Don't say it!" yelled the ant.

"In a—"

"Don't!"

"Rug."

"Aaargh!"

"I can get us out," said the flea quickly.

"Yeah, you and what army?" the ant snickered.

"Here—look," said the flea, and he began to jump up and down on the web.

"What are you doing?" said the ant. "Stop that! Stop doing that!"

But the flea jumped and jumped and did somersaults and flips and the whole web began to shake.

"Stop! We're all going to fall off!" screamed the ant.

And that's exactly what happened.

The ant, the fly, and the flea all plopped out of the trembling web and landed safely on the ground. Well, the fly's wing was a little dented, but at least they were no longer spider food.

"He did it! He did it! The flea did it! He's our hero, he saved us, he did it, the flea did it, he, he . . ." The fly was very excited.

"Yeah, yeah," the ant mumbled.

"C'mon, say it, it won't hurt, say he saved us, c'mon, c'mon," the fly nudged the ant.

There was a moment of silence. The flea was terrified the ant was going to stomp on the fly because he swore he saw smoke coming out of his—well, somewhere. Anyway, after the silence, the ant whispered, "He saved us."

"I can't hear you." The fly nudged again. "A little louder, please."

"HE SAVED US!" the ant bellowed.

"Uh, too loud," the fly said.

"Oh, I'm going to—" The ant turned to the fly and stood straight up, vibrating. This was not good.

"Okay, thank you, wonderful, no problem. Let's go, good idea to get out of here, don't you think?" the flea said, trying to change the subject. "Fly . . . fly us out of here."

"Um, uh, well, my wing is a little bent," the fly said, "and—"

"What about you, Mr. Hero?" the ant asked the flea.

"Oh, my leg. My leg!" the flea whined. "I'd help but it's twisted—"

"All right! Enough! Both of you, get on that leaf," instructed the ant.

The ant tied a strand of spider's web to a leaf. Then, with the fly and the flea sitting on it, the ant began to walk, pulling the leaf behind him.

"Wow," said the flea. "This ant has muscles."
He wasn't sure ants had muscles, but the fly
knew what he meant.

Hours passed. The ant pulled and walked, pulled and walked. And, to take his mind off all the pulling and walking, he asked the flea, "Flea, where did you learn how to do that flippin' stuff? You know, the stuff you were doing on the spider's web."

"I used to be in the circus," said the flea.

"The circus? The *circus*?" The fly was impressed.

"A flea circus," said the flea. "But I
ran away."

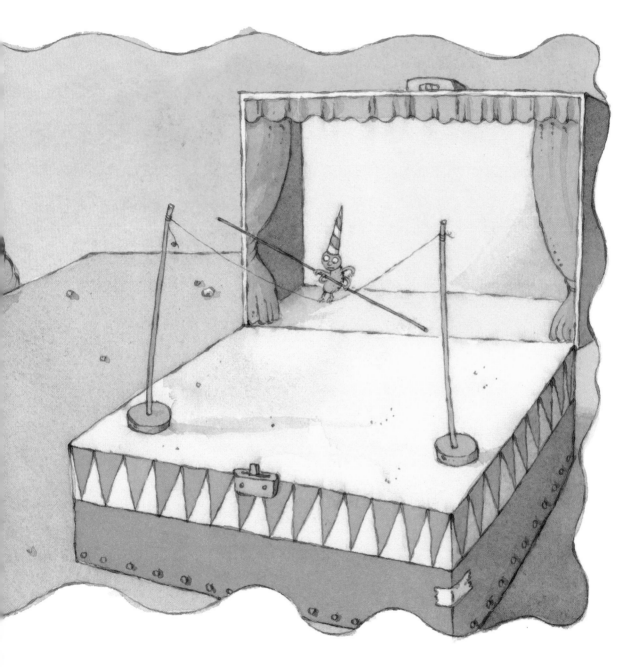

"Wait a minute," said the ant. "What do you mean, you ran away *from* the circus? You're supposed to run away *to* the circus! Everybody runs away TO the circus!"

"I fled," said the flea.

"He's a flea that fled the flea circus," said the fly.

"Even when I was a little flea, I wanted to flee, and I tried to get other fleas to flee with me, but I was the only flea that wanted to flee."

"Makes sense to me," said the fly.

"You see," said the flea, "I want to be a violinist. So fleeing—"

"Stop!" yelled the ant. "I can't take it."

"That's just what I said," said the flea. "I can't take it anymore."

"Makes sense," said the fly.

"Big Jim from Jim's Flea Circus would tie me to a cart and make me run around. Then I'd have to do flips and jump over a lit matchstick and stuff like that. After the shows he'd chain me up. I had to flee."

"Makes—"

"Don't say it," said the ant. "I mean it!"

"Okay, okay," said the fly. "When he says he means it, he means it," he told the flea.

"Makes sense," said the flea.

"That's it. I'm not going another step with you two," said the ant. And he stopped right then and there.

"Please," pleaded the flea. "We have to keep going. Big Jim might be coming after me, and we don't want to end up in that circus!

"They'd throw us in a jar with holes on top . . . and who knows what would happen to us!" The flea was shaking like a leaf, not that all leaves shake but—oh, never mind.

"Calm down. We're nowhere near the circus—" the ant started to say, but stopped because the flea suddenly stood frozen, like a statue.

"What are you doing?" asked the ant.

"Listen! Do you hear that?" asked the flea.

"Hear what? I don't hear anything," replied the ant.

"Me neither," said the fly. "I mean, I hear *you*. Is that what you mean?"

"No! The music!" said the flea.

"Music? I don't hear any—" the ant began.

"Oh, no!" the flea cried. "It's circus music! It's *flea* circus music! We went the wrong way! We went the wrong way! Run for your lives!"

"Don't be ridiculous," said the ant. "I know where we're going and we're nowhere near—"

But before the ant could finish, in one swoop, the ant, the fly, and the flea were all scooped up in Big Jim's palm and whisked away to Jim's Flea Circus.

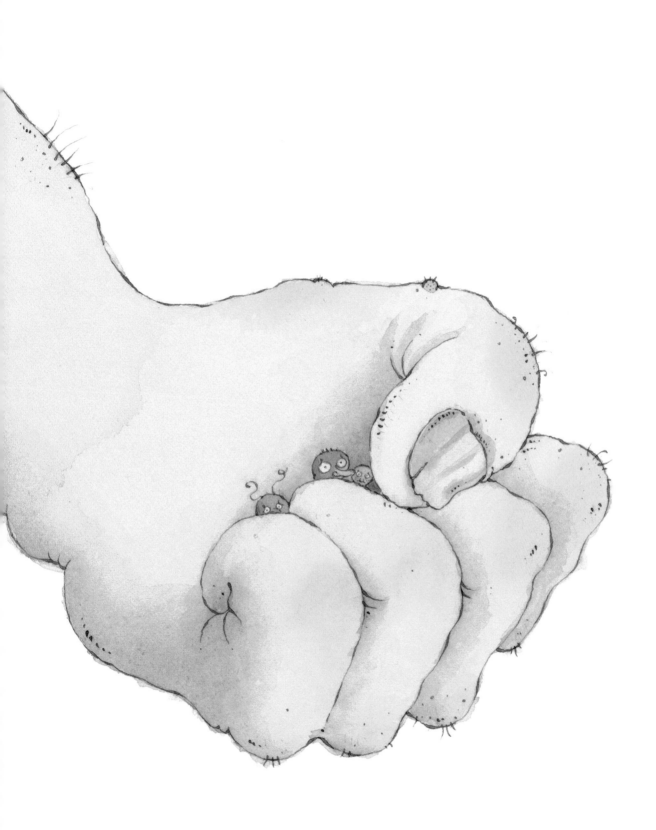

"What an act! You've never seen anything like it!" Big Jim announced.

"Presenting . . . The Ant, The Fly, and The Flea!"

There they were, all three of them, performing six nights a week and twice on Sundays.

Yes, stuck . . . like bugs in a . . .

"Don't say it!"

rug.